D1541024

The Lean Mean Machine

A STORY ABOUT HANDLING FEELINGS

Written by
JOY BERRY

WORD INC.
Waco, Texas 76796

About the Author and Publisher

Joy Berry's mission in life is to help families cope with everyday problems and to help children become competent, responsible, happy individuals. To achieve her goal, she has written over two hundred self-help books for children from birth through age twelve. Her work revolutionized children's publishing by providing families with practical, how-to, living skills information that was previously unavailable in children's books.

Joy gathered a dedicated team of experts, including psychologists, educators, child developmentalists, writers, designers, and artists, to form her publishing company and to help produce her work.

The company, Living Skills Press, produces thoroughly researched books and audio-visual materials that successfully combine humor and education to teach subjects ranging from how to clean a bedroom to how to resolve problems and get along with other people.

Copyright © 1987 by Joy Berry
Living Skills Press, Sebastopol, CA
All rights reserved.
Printed in the United States of America.

Managing Editor: Ellen Klarberg
Copy Editor: Kate Dickey
Contributing Editors: Marilyn Berry, Libby Byers,
Donna Fisher, Michael McBride, Gretchen Savidge
Editorial Assistant: Sandy Passarino

Art Director: Laurie Westdahl
Design: Laurie Westdahl
Production: Caroline Rennard
Illustration design: Bartholomew
Inker: Berenice Happé Iriks
Colorer: Berenice Happé Iriks
Composition: Dwan Typography

Published by Word Incorporated in cooperation with Living Skills Press.

Hello, my name is Joy, and I'd like to tell you a story about Maggie and a valuable lesson she learned about handling uncomfortable feelings.

"Let's not forget that winning isn't everything!" Pamela warned.

Maggie responded with a chuckle, "Oh, my gosh, Pamela, winning isn't everything, but it sure beats the heck out of losing!"

"And win is exactly what we're gonna do!" A.J. added.

"All right!" Teddy shouted as he slapped the palms of A.J.'s hands.

Casey, also ecstatic with the prospects of winning, tried to stifle his giggling, but his enthusiasm could not be contained. There had not been *this* much excitement around the Human Race Club tree house for a long time.

The single object that had charged the air with what seemed like pure electricity had been appropriately named the Lean Mean Machine.

The Lean Mean Machine was a wooden, motorless go-cart that had been carefully constructed by the Human Race Club. It took the group a little more than three months to gather all of the vehicle's many parts and assemble them.

As the club members stood in tribute around the magnificent go-cart, they fondly reminisced about everything that had taken place in the course of the last few months.

Teddy spoke in reverent tones, "Can you believe what we just accomplished? Look at that go-cart, and it's all because we worked together as a team. As far as I'm concerned, we should feel proud of ourselves."

The club members showed their approval of Teddy's remarks by cheering enthusiastically.

When things finally calmed down, Casey asked innocently, "Gee, since this go-cart was such a team effort, how are we going to decide who gets to drive it in tomorrow's race?"

The race Casey referred to was the "Hometown Go-Cart Derby," held annually on the town's steepest hill. Its paved street was closed off one day a year so the special event could take place. Cash prizes were awarded to the winners.

According to an announcement in a local newspaper, $200 would be given to this year's first-place winner, $100 would be given for second place and $50 for third.

Maggie confidently answered Casey's question, "Everybody already knows who's driving in tomorrow's race!"

A.J. broke into the conversation, "Oh yeah! *Who?*"

Maggie ignored A.J.'s question and continued talking, "Don't you remember who came up with the idea of building a go-cart?"

Maggie's comment triggered Pamela's thinking. "Hmmm, the answer to that question would require a bit of research. After all, go-carts have been in existence for years!"

Maggie quickly attacked Pamela's train of thought. "That's not what I mean, Pamela! I'm talking about the person who suggested that we build a go-cart! If you remember, *I* saw the newspaper article, *I* told you guys about it, and *I* suggested that we enter the Derby. That's why *I* should be the one to drive in tomorrow's race!"

It was as though Maggie had set off a string of firecrackers in the middle of the gathering. The group exploded into a series of arguments. Each club member was yelling why he or she should be the one to drive in the Derby.

Only Pamela remained silent. She tried to block out the bickering by putting her hands over her ears, but it was no use. Finally, when she could stand it no longer, she jumped into the middle of the group and yelled as loud as she could, "Everyone listen to me!"

The sound of Pamela's shrill voice stunned everyone into silence.

"Golly, Pamela, I never knew *you* could yell so loudly," Casey said respectfully.

Then it was quiet again.

Pamela took advantage of the silence and continued, "This decision must be made exactly as we make all our decisions. We need to discuss it and then vote on it."

"Pamela's right! Let's go into the tree house and settle this disagreement in a civilized manner!" Teddy said.

The club members were climbing into the tree house when Teddy's mother called out to them. "Teddy, Maggie's mother just phoned. She wants Maggie to come home for her piano lesson."

"Oh, rats! I hate those stupid piano lessons!" Maggie said angrily.

Pamela tried to calm Maggie down. "Maggie, your lesson is only 30 minutes long. Why don't you come back when it's over?"

Teddy chimed in, "That's a good idea. We won't make any major decisions while you're gone. OK, Maggie?"

"Oh, well! I guess that's what I'll have to do. See you guys later."

Reluctantly, Maggie left.

When Maggie came back to the tree house, almost an hour later, she found a note posted on the door. It read, "We went to buy some stuff to eat. Will be back soon."

Maggie decided to wait for the club members to return.

As Maggie wandered impatiently around the tree house, she came across the notebook that contained the club minutes. It lay open to a page of notes that Pamela had written that day. Maggie skimmed through the words. When she got to the last sentence on the page, she shook her head in disbelief.

The sentence read, "In regard to the derby, it was decided that Teddy would be the one . . ."

Maggie could feel her blood beginning to boil as she talked
out loud to herself, "So they weren't going to make any
major decisions without me, huh?"

She threw the notebook down and paced around the tree
house like a tiger in a cage.

The more she thought about the situation, the angrier Maggie became. Finally she climbed down from the tree house and walked over to the Lean Mean Machine. She grabbed the rope that was attached and pulled the go-cart to the sidewalk in front of Teddy's house.

"Nobody is going to tell *me* I can't drive in the Derby. I'll show them!" Maggie said through clenched teeth.

She climbed into the go-cart, and immediately it began to roll. As the Lean Mean Machine picked up speed, Maggie realized that she was losing control of it.

The go-cart was heading toward the big oak tree at the end of the block when Maggie, panic-stricken, let go of the steering wheel and crouched down in the driver's seat.

Seconds later Maggie felt a tremendous thud as the Lean Mean Machine crashed into the oak tree.

A stunned Maggie crawled out of the go-cart to survey the damage. "Oh, no!" she moaned.

Maggie knew immediately that the go-cart's right front wheel was beyond repair.

Quickly, she turned the go-cart around and began dragging it back to the tree house. Luckily, no one was there to see her returning the wounded vehicle to its original place.

She had just finished positioning the go-cart to hide the damage when she heard a familiar voice. It was A.J.'s.

"Well, if it isn't the Human Race Club's very own concert pianist!"

The club members chuckled at A.J.'s remark and waited for Maggie to respond. Surprisingly, she said nothing. After a long uncomfortable pause, Teddy suggested, "Let's get back to our meeting."

Once again the club members assembled together in the tree house. Teddy was the first to speak.

"Maggie, I know I promised we wouldn't make any major decisions while you were gone, but we just couldn't wait for you to get back. Pamela, would you please read the minutes of our meeting to Maggie?"

Pamela opened the notebook to the fateful page that Maggie had read. She began reading the last sentence on the page.

"In regard to the Derby, it was decided that Teddy would be the one . . ." Pamela paused long enough to turn the page, and then she continued, ". . . to get the Lean Mean Machine to the race, and Maggie will be the one to drive it!"

All eyes turned toward Maggie, but instead of seeing the wildly excited person they expected to see, the club members saw a sullen Maggie sitting in silence, staring at the floor.

After a few moments Casey said, "Gee whiz, Maggie, we thought you wanted to be the one to drive in the Derby."

Maggie solemnly rose to her feet and motioned for the club members to follow her. She led them out of the tree house to where the go-cart stood.

When Maggie pointed to the crumpled wheel, everyone gasped in horror. Casey was the first to blurt out, "What happened?"

Fighting back the tears, Maggie told her sad, embarrassing story. When she finally finished, she broke into sobs.

"I shouldn't have gotten so angry!" Maggie wailed.

Pamela put her arm around Maggie in an effort to reassure her. "There's nothing wrong with getting angry. We all get angry once in a while."

"Yeah, like right now I feel pretty angry about that bent-up wheel!" A.J. said.

Teddy nudged A.J. and whispered, "Be quiet! Can't you see how upset Maggie is?"

Reflecting on Pamela's remarks, Casey added, "Joy always says there is no such thing as a bad feeling. There are only bad ways to handle feelings."

Soon it became obvious the meeting was over. As the club members left the tree house, they vowed they would have their go-cart repaired and ready for next year's Derby.

Meanwhile, the Lean Mean Machine took on a whole new meaning. Sitting beneath the tree house, the go-cart served as a constant reminder of what can happen when emotions are not handled properly. This message had cost the Human Race Club $200, and only time would tell whether or not they got their money's worth.

So what can *we* learn from all of this?

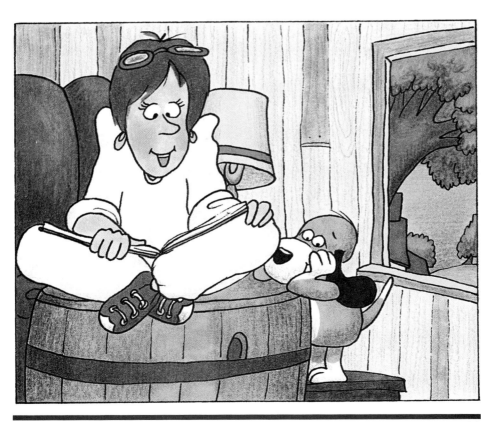

Maggie learned the hard way that uncomfortable feelings can cause a lot of problems if they are not handled properly.

There are several things Maggie could have done to prevent the disaster that was a result of her uncontrolled anger.

Obviously, Maggie did not realize that a decision affecting a group of people needs the approval of the entire group.

Maggie had no right to assume that she would be driving the go-cart in the Derby.

This was a decision that should have been made by all of the club members.

Maggie jumped to conclusions too quickly. It is important to have all the facts about something before forming an opinion.

It would have been better for Maggie to give the club members a chance to explain what she had read in Pamela's notebook before she acted on her emotions.

Maggie learned that uncomfortable feelings need to be handled in acceptable ways.

It is *not* acceptable to do anything that would
- hurt yourself,
- hurt others, or
- damage or destroy anyone's property.

EPILOG

The last time I saw the go-cart, it was being fine-tuned for another big derby in a neighboring town. Maggie had re-placed the wheel she had destroyed, and the go-cart looked better than ever.

I wasn't sure whether or not the go-cart would win the race, but I was sure of this: No one in the Human Race Club would ever forget the Lean Mean Machine.

The End